Brother Francis and the Friendly Beasts

Brother Francis and the

Friendly Beasts

Margaret Hodges
Pictures by Ted Lewin

Charles Scribner's Sons · New York
Collier Macmillan Canada · Toronto
Maxwell Macmillan International Publishing Group
New York · Oxford · Singapore · Sydney

For Clare

—M.H.

For Bones and Dundee
and for all of us who talk to animals

—T.L.

In the old Italian town of Assisi, there once lived a boy named
Francis. He was much like any other boy who happened to have a
rich father. Because his father was a merchant who sold fine silks,
Francis wore silk. He wore soft and strong shoes of the best leather.
Because his father had a stable full of horses, Francis rode a spirited
horse. At home he ate what he liked—and plenty of it. Someday he
would become a rich man like his father. There were few rich boys in
Assisi, and many who were poor. They wore rags and walked barefoot.
They begged for bread. But Francis did not think about them—or
care. Eat, drink, and be merry was his rule.

Then one day he fell sick, and while he lay in bed, he began to think. When he was well again in body but still troubled in his mind, he saw beggars along the road and thought how much he had, while they had nothing.

He took some fine silk from his father's shop to sell it in another town. He sold his father's horse, as well, and started home, wondering what was best to do with the money. Near Assisi he saw a tumble-down church and offered its poor priest all that he had. But when the priest heard how Francis had gotten the money, he refused to accept it. Disappointed, Francis left the coins on a windowsill of the church and walked on to Assisi.

His father soon recovered the money, but Francis was in disgrace. His mother wept and his father cursed him. He had given Francis all that he wanted; now he ordered him to give back everything and leave home.

Full of a strange joy, Francis gave back to his father all that he had, even stripping off his fine clothes and leather shoes. He put on a coarse brown robe and tied a rope around his waist. Then, barefoot like the poorest of the poor, he walked away.

From Assisi he tramped along the rough roads, under the sun and the moon, in all kinds of weather, sleeping at night in hillside caves or in shelters made of branches. He worked for his food and begged for bread when he could not find work. But on every country road, he saw the beauty and grace of animals, of birds singing as they flew, of silvery fish darting in clear water. He heard the hum of insects in the roadside grass, and they, too, were beautiful. God was the father of all living things, and all were brothers and sisters. They gave him joy, and he sang for joy as he walked the roads.

Most people thought him strange—so poor, yet singing. Some thought him crazy. They stared and turned away. But many liked his looks, this slim and graceful young man with the strong, sweet voice and the smile, and the fine hands that seemed to bless everything he touched. Soon a few other men joined him and followed the rule that he gave them: "As you travel, take no food or money with you, and give whatever you have to anyone who asks for help." They called themselves brothers as they went, two by two, preaching and helping the poor.

Francis preached to animals as well as to people. Once in some trees by the roadside, he saw a great flock of birds and preached to them. "My little sisters, praise God as you sing, because you can fly wherever you wish. The air holds you up. It belongs to you. God gave you beautiful feathers so that you need not weave or sew. He gave you trees for your homes and fields, and rivers for your food and drink." The birds opened their beaks, stretched their wings, bobbed their heads, and sang to show that they understood.

One evening when Francis and another brother were eating in the open air, a nightingale began to sing close by. Whenever the bird paused, Francis took up the song, and so they went on all night long, singing together, the small brown bird and the man with the bright face under his brown hood.

Even the smallest creatures were worth his love and care. Francis praised the bees for their hard and skillful work. How could such little things build marvelous honeycombs and fill them with sweetness? He put out wine and honey to keep the bees alive through the winter. If he saw a worm on the road, he would pick it up and put it out of harm's way.

One day Francis came to the town of Gubbio, where he heard that a fierce wolf was lurking in the woods outside the city walls, killing sheep in the fields. Fathers and mothers would not let their children out of their sight. They told Francis their trouble, and he pitied them. Then, without fear, he walked to the edge of the woods and called, "Come to me, Brother Wolf."

The terrified people watched from the city gate and saw a wonderful thing. The wolf ran out of the woods toward Francis, snarling, ready to attack. But Francis stood still and said, "Brother Wolf, do not harm me or anyone else here." The wolf lay down and seemed to listen.

"Brother Wolf," said Francis, "you have done much damage here, killing animals and even people, but I know that you were hungry. Now, Brother Wolf, if these people promise to feed you, will you promise not to harm them or their animals?" The wolf nodded his head and put his paw in Francis's hand as a sign that he would keep his promise. Then he followed Francis peacefully to the city gate of Gubbio, where the people waited in wonder.

From that time on, they fed the wolf every day and he went about the town like a friendly dog. When he died of old age, the people of Gubbio missed him as if he had always been a friend.

But much as Francis liked the wild creatures, the farm animals and
birds were his favorites: the quiet oxen, the patient donkeys, nesting
doves, sheep grazing in the fields. He loved the farm children. If a little
one fell and hurt his knee, Francis would carry him home as a good
shepherd carries a lamb.

One evening, not long before Christmas, Francis and another brother were on their way toward the little town of Greccio, where Francis had many friends, both rich and poor. They met a few late travelers on the road. Shepherds lay half asleep among their flocks, and only the shepherd dogs raised their heads as the brothers went by. On such a night as this, Francis thought, shepherds had watched over their flocks while a man named Joseph followed the road to Bethlehem with his wife, Mary.

Everyone must want to be in Bethlehem on Christmas Eve, thought Francis, but the people of Greccio could not travel so far. Suddenly Francis saw a way to make Bethlehem come to Greccio.

The brothers hurried on to the house of a good man named John, who was their friend. He owned land for miles around and knew all the peasants. He had given Francis a mountainside with a cave, where the brothers often rested, looking down over the rich valley. In such a cave at Bethlehem, friendly animals had been stabled and the child Jesus was born. Francis told his plan to John and asked for help.

John agreed. He sent word to the townspeople and farmers that they should come to the cave, bringing their children to celebrate Christmas with Brother Francis, who would have a surprise for them.

On Christmas Eve, all the paths from Greccio and the country around about the town were filled with streams of light as men, women, and children walked up to the mountain cave, carrying torches. They were mostly poor folk, laughing and chatting as they climbed the slope, eager to see their old friend Brother Francis.

When they looked into the cave, they fell silent. The light of the torches shone on an ox and a donkey stabled near a manger filled with hay. And in the manger lay a baby. Was this Greccio—or Bethlehem?

Then Brother Francis stepped out of the shadows. He lifted up the baby and put him in the arms of his mother. She was a peasant mother whom everyone knew well, but for a moment, she seemed to be Mary, and the baby, the child of Bethlehem.

Brother Francis read aloud the story of how the child Jesus had been born while shepherds woke in their fields to see the sky filled with bright angels singing "Glory to God in the highest, and on earth, peace and goodwill."

Afterward, everyone went home singing. One by one, the lights went out, and the little town of Greccio slept under the stars.

People said that there had never been anyone quite like Francis, and many stories were told about him. Some are legends that simply show how he loved all living things; they have a truth of their own. Other stories are true in fact, like the story of the Christmas when Francis brought Bethlehem to Greccio.

We know some of his own words. Not long before Francis died, he made a new song:

> Praised be my Lord God for all his creatures; especially
> our Brother Sun, who brings us the day, and the light; he is
> beautiful and shines with a very great splendor.
>
> Praised be my Lord for Sister Moon, and for the stars clear
> and lovely in heaven.
>
> Praised be my Lord for Brother Wind, and cloud, and calms
> and all weather, for God's air gives us life.
>
> Praised be my Lord for Sister Water, who is very helpful to
> us and humble, and precious, and clean.
>
> Praised be my Lord for Brother Fire, who gives us light in
> the darkness; he is bright and pleasant, and mighty, and strong.
>
> Praised be my Lord for Mother Earth, who feeds us and
> protects us and brings forth grass and many fruits and flowers
> of all colors.
>
> Praise and bless the Lord.

*The text for St. Francis's "Canticle of the Sun" is adapted
from the translation by Matthew Arnold.*

Text copyright © 1991 by Margaret Hodges
Illustrations copyright © 1991 by Ted Lewin

Charles Scribner's Sons Books for Young Readers
Macmillan Publishing Company
866 Third Avenue, New York, NY 10022
Collier Macmillan Canada, Inc.
1200 Eglinton Avenue East, Suite 200
Don Mills, Ontario M3C 3N1

10 9 8 7 6 5 4 3 2
Printed in Hong Kong

Library of Congress Cataloging-in-Publication Data
Hodges, Margaret.
Brother Francis and the friendly beasts / Margaret Hodges;
pictures by Ted Lewin. — 1st ed.   p.   cm.
Summary: A young man rejects his wealthy background to lead a life
of poverty and good works, always befriending animals.
1. Francis, of Assisi, Saint, 1182-1226 — Juvenile literature.
2. Christian saints — Italy — Assisi — Biography — Juvenile literature.
[1. Francis, of Assisi, Saint, 1182-1226.   2. Saints.]
I. Lewin, Ted, ill.   II. Title.
BX4700.F69H63   1991   271'.302 — dc20
90-33206   [B]   CIP   AC   ISBN 0-684-19173-3